The Boy Who Ate the Moon

by Christopher King

illustrated by John Wallner

Philomel Books • New York

Text copyright © 1988 by Christopher King.
Illustrations copyright © 1988 by John Wallner.
All rights reserved. Published by Philomel Books,
a division of The Putnam & Grosset Group,
200 Madison Avenue, New York, NY 10016.
Published simultaneously in Canada.
Printed in Hong Kong by South China Printing Co.

Library of Congress Cataloging-in-Publication Data
King, Christopher.   The boy who ate the moon.
Summary: After eating the moon, a boy takes a strange journey.
{1. Moon—Fiction. 2. Fantasy} I. Wallner, John C., ill. II. Title.
PZ7.K5753Bo   1987   {E}   87-2232
ISBN 0-399-21459-3   First Impression

*F*or Matthew, my own boy moon.   C.K.

*T*o Robert Orsini and other children that sail with the moon.   J.C.W.

One cool year when animals still talked and the sky
reached all the way to the ground, there was a quiet
boy, a big-eyed boy with skin the color of a doe.

He was a boy who lived in trees, a boy who sailed the sky in a
great, green ship. He could balance on the high branches like an
eagle and swing down the bending limbs like a chimpanzee.

Usually he did not travel in the trees at night.

But late one Autumn when the wind had just blown the last
leaf off Grandaddy Maple, the moon rose up into the midnight
purple, a silver cookie covered with sugar dust.

Suddenly, it was trapped by bony, wooden fingers and stuffed
into the bowl of the old crow's nest.

It couldn't get out.

The boy knew it was up to him to save the moon and set it
free.

So he climbed out the window as his father said he never
should. He slid down the slate roof as he never dared do.

But as he put one bare foot on the dark elbow of the old tree,
he heard a voice growl:

"Don't do it! Don't do it! Some never return!"

It was Daddy Raccoon, gnawing a soft orange on the leaf pile
below.

But the boy just growled back, and, with a whistle, the bandit
vanished.

Like a tightrope walker up on his toes, the boy balanced his
way across to the thick trunk . . .

stretched his hands up to grab the first branch . . .

when just above his head a purring voice said "Hrrrumph!"

Perched in a notch was a large orange cat. Clearly he heard her
rumble:

"Don't do it! Don't do it! Some never return!"

He just hissed "Scat!" and she scrambled.

Like a sailor he climbed, as the branches came one and one, and they were black and rough and felt good to his fingers. Out of the corner of his eye the house was small, the yard was small, the street was invisible.

Suddenly his hand touched fur. He heard small claws and a brittle voice rattle:

"Don't do it! Don't do it! Some never return!"

It was a fat gray squirrel, upside down on the bark.

But the boy just snapped his teeth, and it ducked around the trunk.

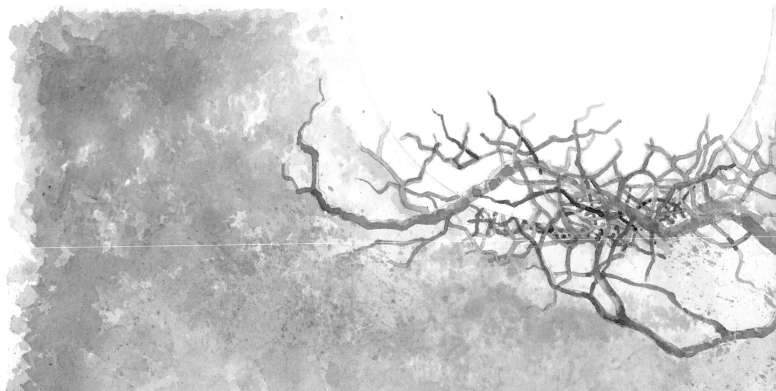

Now he crept on all fours, out along the branch that held the moon so tight. Smooth and slippery, it bobbed and twisted under his toes.

Then he reached up for that glowing circle, just to give it a little push to set it free. It wouldn't budge. But he felt a silvery shock and saw that his fingers were coated—just lightly—with moon sugar.

He put them in his mouth.

They tasted like moon magic, like all the sweet things the moon had ever seen in its circle round the world:

Ripe mangos from India, chocolates from English shopwindows, trays of sweets in Africa and wild strawberries from his own back door meadow.

Without knowing how, he found himself sitting in the old crow's nest with the moon in his lap. He ate it, and he ate it, and he ate it until it was all inside him, except for one small piece which melted out of his fingers, floated down like a firefly and was snapped out of the air by Daddy Raccoon.

But now he was so full he was sleepy and light with moon dreams. The moon, though eaten, was still full of floating.

And caught by Great West Wind that always blows around the earth, he was lifted beyond the treetops and rose up into the cool, dark sky.

He woke when a vee of geese flew by, so close he could feel the breeze of their wings on his face.

Below him a great city spread out a quilt of lights.

And then he knew!

"I am the moon!" he shouted, "Look at me!" He kicked out at a passing cloud.

Suddenly he was tumbling head over heels across the sky!

He rolled and tumbled, tumbled and rolled, across vast black plains, so fast he was breathless, never knowing up from down.

He rolled and tumbled, tumbled and rolled, now across great green seas where the white manes of the sea stallions tossed as they pawed their wet hooves at the moon.

He rolled and tumbled, tumbled and rolled, over the white ice of glaciers, over hot lands of dark dragon green, over deserts in terrible silence.

Then, over a mighty forest, he was pushed right into a cold, wet snow cloud.

It was the wind in his eyes that made the boymoon cry when he tried to turn toward home.

"Will I ever return?" he sighed.

Then suddenly, mountains with peaks as sharp as spider's teeth
loomed right in front of him!

Quickly, he twirled his arms, changed the way he was going,
and rolled right around them.

"I can go around!" he shouted.

"Go around!" the valleys echoed.

"Go around!" the mountains rumbled.

And now he knew how to get home.

He rolled and tumbled, spun and somersaulted, whirled and cartwheeled beyond huts and houses, castles and pyramids, spires and skyscrapers, around and around, chasing the horizon into the morning.

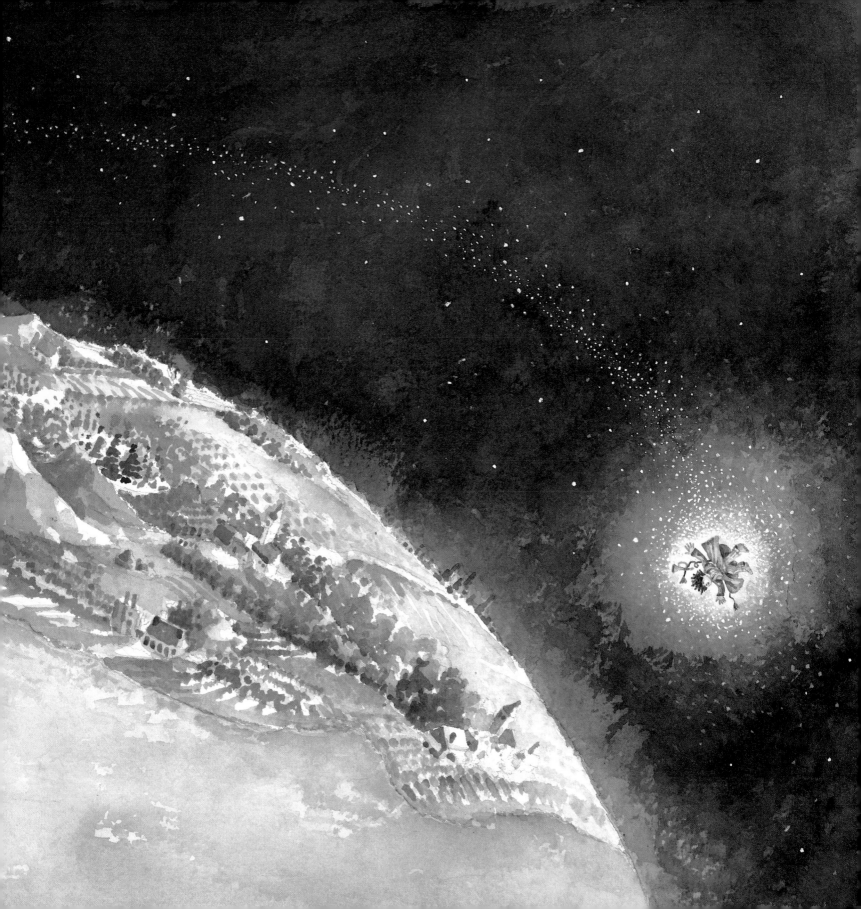

Now the sun threw off its blanket of darkness and turned the sky blue and more blue until it was so light that the moon grew thin and thinner inside him.

A last gust pushed the boy into the branches of the same Old Maple where his journey had begun, and the moon's last slim wafer slipped out of him and faded away.

He didn't remember climbing down, but he must have done it,
because the next time he opened his eyes, the sun was warm on
the side of his face, and he was lying at the roots of the tree,
cradled in his father's lap.

The orange cat walked past and yawned.

The boy looked up at his father's drowsy face.

"Some do return," he said, in a whisper, "if they just find out
how."